BRITTON
39815 Burton Drive
Rancho Mirage, CA. 92270

760 - 898 - 4052

# THE HLE STORY

BY

## RUTHIE DARLING

ILLUSTRATED BY

## TRICIA COTTENGAIM

ARK PUBLISHERS
PRINTED IN THE U.S.A.

Gassner, Ruth
Darling, Ruthie

THE HOLE STORY BY RUTHIE DARLING
ILLUSTRATED BY TRICIA COTTENGAIM
1ST EDITION.
FIRST PRINTING 2009
ISBN: 978-0-578-03061-6

Library of Congress Control Number: 2008910133

**ARK Publishers**
P.O. Box 10051
Palm Desert, CA 92260
www.RuthieDarling.com
RuthieDarling8@aol.com

H is for holes - old and new
and here are some HOLES

I'm sharing with you!

There's a hole in my donut,
but soon it won't be here,

'cause when I eat my donut up
the hole will disappear!

A moth ate a hole
in my red long-sleeved sweater,

but when Mom sewed it up
I felt a lot better!

There are holes in the buttons
that are sewn onto my clothes,

this includes my nice, white sweater
that has buttons like a rose!

My Mom's shoes have holes
in lots of different places,

but my sneakers have ten holes
for long and fancy laces!

**T**-shirts and pants
come with holes when they're new,
that my head and my arms
and my legs all go through!

I have a soft blanket
I sleep with at night,
it has lots of holes
and it's really a sight!

**M**om sewed up the hole
in my big stuffed brown bear ...
a hole that started
as one tiny tear!

My shower head has holes
and sticks out from the wall,
but I can't take a shower yet
because I am too small!

**M**y sprinkling can has holes -
how many I don't know,
but I love to sprinkle water
'cause it helps the flowers grow!

I have fun digging holes
when I get to play in sand ...
I can use my plastic shovel
and sometimes I use both hands!

Every bottle has a hole
made to drink from or to pour,
Mom lets me choose one bottle
when we are at the store!

There's a ball that has three holes
which I stick my fingers in,

and when I get to throw the ball ...
sometimes I knock down pins!

NOPQRSTUVWXYZ

**DAYS**

Sunday
Monday
Tuesday
Wednesday
Thursday
Friday
Saturday

**MONTHS**

January
February
March
April
May
June

July
August
September
October
November
December

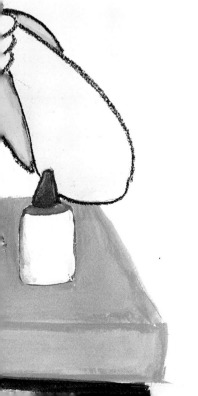

The letters of the alphabet
have lots of holes, too,
big and small - I like them all,
but my favorite one is Q!

**M**y nose has two holes
for air to go through,

and when I catch a cold
my nose goes **AH-CHOO!!**

I also have two holes -
a small one in each ear,

but I don't get to see them
when they're covered by my hair!

My balloon has a hole
that my Dad filled with air,
and when he was finished -
he tied it to my chair!

**W**ell, I've looked all around
and I'm done for today,
but I hope you look for **holes**
when you go outside to play!

## About the Author

Ruthie Darling is a former Elementary Grade School Teacher who has been inspired by children throughout her life. She is passionate about all forms of creative self-expression and pursuing the Arts continues to fill her soul and capture her spirit. Look for *"The One Stop Pet Shop: More Than a Cat and a Dog and a Frog on a Log"* - coming in the near future.

## About the Illustrator

Tricia Cottengaim, a graduate of Cal State San Bernadino with a Bachelors of Arts in Painting, is currently pursuing her Elementary Education Teaching Credential. She loves creating art of any kind and has always admired the imagination of children.